Pete the Cat
Checks Out the Library

by James Dean

HARPER FESTIVAL

An Imprint of HarperCollinsPublishers

Harperfestival is an imprint of HarperCollins Publishers.
Pete the Cat Checks Out the Library
Copyright © 2018 by James Dean
Pete the Cat is a registered trademark of Pete the Cat, LLC.

Library of Congress Control Number: 2018938257
ISBN 978-0-06-267532-3

Typography by Honee Jang
18 19 20 21 22 SCP 10 9 8 7 6 5 4 3 2 1
❖
First Edition

Pete's mom is taking him to the library for the first time.
The librarian gives Pete his very own library card.
"Cool!" says Pete.
The librarian smiles. "Time for the tour!"

The librarian takes Pete through the library.
There is a big desk where people wait to check out books.

Pete sees some of his friends reading at a long table.
It's very peaceful and quiet. How relaxing!

The librarian takes Pete to her favorite room.
There are lots of Pete-size chairs and tables and shelves.
There are books of every shape, size, and color.

"What do I do now?" Pete asks.

"Now you read a book," the librarian says.

"Which book should I read?" asks Pete.

"You can read any book you like," says the librarian.

Pete looks around. There are so many books!

Pete picks up a book all about
airplanes and jets.

He reads it and pretends he is a stunt pilot.
He flies a super-fast jet and does loop-the-loops
and spirals high in the sky!

Then Pete finds a book with dragons, wizards, and unicorns on the cover.

He reads it and imagines that he is a powerful wizard, using magic spells and a special wand to defend his castle against a fire-breathing dragon.

Next Pete opens up a book about spiders and insects. He reads it and imagines that he is a scientist studying all types of critters in the wild.

BUGS

He has to be very still to study some critters . . .

and very fast to study others.

Then Pete chooses a book with all sorts of scary monsters on the cover. It is a book of fairy tales.

MONSTERS

Pete reads it and pretends that he is in a dark, spooky forest trying to outsmart a big, bad wolf.

Pete puts that book back on the shelf—it is too scary!

Pete opens up a book about the pyramids in Egypt. He reads it and pretends that he is an explorer riding a camel across the desert . . .

and climbing to the top of a giant pyramid.

Next Pete picks a book with all sorts of robots on the cover.
He reads it and imagines that he is a robot at a robot dance party.

His arms and legs make whizzing sounds when he moves.
When Robot Pete speaks he says,

"Bleep. Bloop. Bleep!"

Next Pete picks up a book about superheroes.
He reads it and makes believe that he is a superhero.

He flies around the city in a colorful cape chasing bad guys and saving the day.

Then Pete spots a big book about the
ocean and all its creatures.
  He reads it and imagines that he is
a scientist in a submarine deep in the
Atlantic Ocean, looking for whales,
squids, and sharks.

There are so many wonderful books to read at the library.
Pete can be whatever he imagines with a book.

Reading is super groovy!